Nene's Tales Part II

Ancel Mondia

Ukiyoto Publishing

All global publishing rights are held by

Ukiyoto Publishing

Published in 2023

Content Copyright © Ancel Mondia

ISBN 9789360161248

*All rights reserved.
No part of this publication may be reproduced, transmitted, or stored in a retrieval system, in any form by any means, electronic, mechanical, photocopying, recording or otherwise, without the prior permission of the publisher.*

The moral rights of the authors have been asserted.

This is a work of fiction. Names, characters, businesses, places, events, locales, and incidents are either the products of the author's imagination or used in a fictitious manner. Any resemblance to actual persons, living or dead, or actual events is purely coincidental.

This book is sold subject to the condition that it shall not by way of trade or otherwise, be lent, resold, hired out or otherwise circulated, without the publisher's prior consent, in any form of binding or cover other than that in which it is published.

www.ukiyoto.com

Contents

Flynn the Fly	1
Camille the Clam	6
Liza the Lizard	11
Salome the Salmon	17
Bea the Bee	22
Tita the Tick	28
About the Author	33

Flynn the Fly

In an impoverished and chaotic slum, an untidy girl gradually grew into a naive lady in her deteriorating shelter, next to that of a stubborn man whom she dearly kept as her secret love since their innocent childhood. Her bulgy eyes creepily stared at him each time he casually passed by her. The nonchalant man normally ignored the timid lady, but the time suddenly came when he shamelessly expressed his annoyance towards her.

"Why do you keep on looking at me, Flynn?! Do you like me?!" He abruptly blurted.

Flynn unexpectedly blushed in embarrassment as if she completely failed to consciously think that her romantic feelings had been totally obvious to her childhood love. The appalling confrontation extremely stupefied her and she confusingly gave a suggestive reaction.

"Yes. No. I mean, is it wrong to look at you, Gwynn?" She shyly stuttered.

Gwynn naturally had an emotionless face that apparently deprived Flynn to precisely see through him. But he simply shook his head and quickly waved his hand, and she quietly responded by slowly nodding her head.

"Forget it." He calmly spoke.

"I will." She timidly replied.

Gwynn genuinely smiled to fully lighten up the intense atmosphere, and Flynn obviously felt at ease in his delightful presence.

"I have a job now in the city. I sell fruits. And they call me a vendor." He happily talked.

"That's good for you." She said with a smile.

"Thanks. Well, I have to go now." He hurriedly spoke.

Flynn simply nodded her head, and Gwynn swiftly turned his back.

In her filthy shelter, Flynn normally daydreamed about strongly having a sweet relationship with Gwynn. She clearly imagined embracing his hard body and kissing his soft lips. She even visualized herself intensely making love with him. She was deeply savoring her secret visions, when a familiar voice abruptly interrupted her.

"Flynn! Flynn! Are you there?" Gwynn loudly shouted.

Her bulgy eyes suddenly widened when she eventually recognized the masculine voice of her childhood love. She swiftly opened her creaking door, and warmly welcomed him.

"It's you, Gwynn. Come in." She spoke in delight.

Gwynn cheerfully grinned as he abruptly lifted his hands that were holding filled paper bags.

"What are those?" Flynn asked in curiosity.

"These are fruits! I'm giving them to you." He charmingly said.

Gwynn apparently looked innocent, but Flynn suddenly appeared suggestive. She intensely stared at him, but he confusingly remained quiet. Flynn gradually grew impatient as he slowly looked uncomfortable.

"Are you courting me?" She shamelessly asked.

"No!" He quickly replied.

"So why are you giving me those fruits?" She queried in disappointment.

"They are overripe. And I don't want them to rot." He innocently explained.

All of a sudden, Flynn forcefully grabbed the filled paper bags from his weak hands. Gwynn abruptly appeared emotionless, and Flynn slowly became timid.

"I accept these because they come from you. Thank you." She shyly spoke.

Without waiting for his response, she rapidly closed her creaking door.

As days passed by, Flynn gradually noticed that Gwynn grew distant from her. She repeatedly tried to casually get his attention, by intentionally standing before him, and loudly calling his name. But Gwynn purposefully ignored Flynn, until the time suddenly came when she boldly confronted him.

"What's wrong, Gwynn? Why are you ignoring me?" She painfully asked.

He offensively blurted. "I have a girlfriend! I don't want to give her any reason to get jealous."

There was pain in her eyes as there was guilt in his.

"You're lying, Gwynn." She weakly sobbed.

"I will marry her. I love her." He clearly admitted.

Flynn slowly entered her deteriorating shelter and shut her creaking door.

As days passed by, Flynn became thin and pale as if she was severely suffering from a mysterious illness. The time suddenly came when she disappeared without any trace, and her presence was replaced by insects with bulgy eyes that ordinarily flew in the slum and were seemingly attracted to rotten fruits.

Camille the Clam

An old man habitually visited a typical bay at dawn that normally held the presence of the dark, the feeling of chill, and the ambience of calm.

He leisurely relished the early morning by quietly expecting a new spark of exhilarating idea to intensely fuel his literary narrative.

His momentary wait suddenly concluded with a familiar strike, as stimulating flashes of living memories spontaneously surfaced, and extremely revived his hidden emotions of romance.

His mysterious energy of love felt like watery substances that freely flowed upon his waking state of physical being, as his creative juices strongly flowed through his nonmaterial existence.

It seemed that the sole help he gravely needed was to let his black ink effortlessly bleed his persisting words, so the secret experiences within him would be privately washed away.

His suppressed truth disturbingly screamed for liberating expression, when he suddenly underwent an internal break of dawn upon blissfully seeing his longtime love.

The typical bay that ordinarily existed as his favorite place gradually transformed as the calm turned into zeal, the chill into warmth, and the dark into light.

The old woman before him was like the heavenly moon to his human existence that was comparable to the organic globe.

He constantly gravitated to her, as the natural satellite in boundless space normally caused rising and falling tides in water-bodies of the living earth.

His love approached him in a slow pace, as her light steps inspired him to envision her happily walking down the aisle toward the sacred altar, where he was emotionally standing.

She radiantly smiled and softly spoke before him. "You look dreamy, Clinton."

Her feminine voice startled him in a second, and he quickly regained his masculine composure.

She continued in curiosity. "What were you thinking?"

Clinton confusingly shook his head and stammered. "Nothing."

The woman subtly looked unconvinced, but instantly shrugged off her doubts.

"You're here again. As usual. Were you looking for your muse again?" She asked with anticipation.

Clinton seemed to have second thoughts before he was able to answer. "Yes."

She slowly stared at the tranquil waters, as sadness was clearly reflected in her charming eyes.

"I am jealous of this bay. I wish I was this bay. Or even just a part of it. So somehow, I can be your muse." She painfully whispered to herself.

Clinton obviously noticed her trembling lips and wondered about her inaudible words.

"What were you saying, Camille?" He asked in curiosity.

"You just can't love anything. I think this bay is so special to you. That's why this is your muse." She boldly spoke despite her cowardice to her real emotions.

Clinton loudly talked inside his head while his lips were actually firmly closed. "It's not the bay that I keep visiting. It's you, Camille."

Two connected old souls were close together at the typical bay, but they constantly felt that they were miles away from each other, exactly like the moon and the earth.

But despite the enormous distance between the two heavenly bodies, the moon was able to cause high tides in the earth.

Clinton suddenly spoke. "See me tomorrow. Here. At the same time."

Camille confusingly answered. "You don't have to say that. We always meet here. At the same time."

He continued with hesitation. "It will be different tomorrow. I will tell you something."

Clinton immediately turned his back and walked away, but Camille stood still with doubts and pain in her face.

Twenty-four hours were finally gone, and Clinton quietly arrived at the typical bay, with the resolve to confess his hidden love.

But something unusual alarmingly happened, Camille was completely out of sight.

Heavy tears freely fell from his sorrowful eyes, as if he clearly understood the unfavorable situation.

In extreme heartbreak, he spoke. "You told me. Only death could separate us. But you didn't tell me. That it would be today."

Clinton knelt down on the sand, as he slowly witnessed the low tide that made him strongly feel the disturbing absence of his longtime love.

"I never told you. You are my muse, Camille." He confessed with failed hopes in his heart.

He gradually noticed shelled creatures on the sand that he saw for the first time. He gently picked one of them, tightly held it close to his chest, and resoundingly sobbed.

Liza the Lizard

The stillness in a vast and dense bamboo forest was suddenly disturbed by a man that crazily ran with a palpitating heart. He desperately attempted to escape another man that swiftly chased him with a sharp dagger in his forceful hand.

The defeated weak runner was mightily caught by the victorious fierce chaser. Despite the determined resistance of the exhausted victim, the beastly attacker robustly stabbed his vulnerable target in the leg.

The wounded man alarmingly groaned, and the dried leaves on the loamy ground noisily rustled as an apparent signal of a potential witness. The conscious attacker instantly fled from the crime scene and nonchalantly left his bleeding victim.

A young woman surprisingly showed up before the crawling pained victim. She quickly studied the eerie area, and gently knelt down to closely see the bleeding wound of the fatigued man.

The composed woman acted like an aider by suddenly pulling out a plain handkerchief and attentively wrapped the stabbed leg of her poor patient.

The aided man surprisingly heard the feminine voice of his gentle lifesaver as she softly spoke. "I need to bring you home."

The young woman deliberately placed her smooth arms around his exhausted body to strongly support him to weakly stand, and they gradually left the eerie area.

They leisurely walked a few meters and consciously stopped in front of a bamboo house. They quietly entered through the rustic door, and casually began a superficial conversation inside.

The wounded man meekly sat in a wooden chair, and suddenly spoke in a low voice. "Thank you for saving my life."

The female homeowner simply nodded and mindfully filled a light washbowl with clear water. She slowly untied her bloodstained handkerchief around his bleeding leg to gently rinse his fresh wound.

The aided man asked in curiosity. "What should I call you?"

The young woman abruptly lifted her head and stared straight to his stunned eyes as she coldly answered. "Liza."

Her masculine patient mutely took a few seconds before he confusingly spoke again. "I am Liam. Thank you for helping me."

Liza firmly asked. "Who did this to you?"

Liam replied with hesitation. "An enemy."

Her brow and voice raised at once. "Obviously!"

He startled and stammered. "I can't tell you. I don't know you yet. Though you helped me."

Her face and eyes calmed. "I only helped you because I wish to be a healer. I believe it is my purpose to help heal others."

Liam attentively nodded and sincerely spoke. "Thank you for letting me know. I know you'll be a good healer."

Liza sweetly smiled with hopeful eyes. "Thank you, Liam."

He subtly smiled. "You're welcome, Liza."

Days normally passed by as Liam peacefully stayed in Liza's bamboo house. As his wound in the leg slowly healed, his relationship with her deepened.

Liam consciously recalled their first conversation and abruptly brought it up one evening.

"Liza, I'm sorry for hiding the truth from you. I refused to tell you about an enemy."

She was utterly surprised and quietly listened to him.

He clearly continued to talk without intended interruption from her.

"I am the son of the owner of this bamboo forest. From a nearby country, I came here to claim my inheritance. But another man also claimed this land because he is a native of this place."

Her eyes bulged in confusion and shame, and her lips remained tightly closed.

Liam romantically stared at Liza as he comforted her with loving words.

"You have nothing to worry about, Liza. Mine is yours as well. I know you thought no one owns this land so you built a house here. But your house is our house."

Liza spoke in relief and gratitude. "Thank you, Liam."

All of a sudden, loud knocks on the rustic door were clearly heard. Liza swiftly stood and opened it, and an unknown man appeared before her.

In a second, Liam shockingly caught the falling woman. Liza was in Liam's trembling arms as her delicate neck was profusely bleeding.

The beastly attacker proudly growled. "This land is all mine. And mine will never be yours."

Liam was extremely stupefied as his teary eyes were strongly fixed on the dying woman. Liza weakly whispered as she painfully gasped.

"I'm not sure if I can heal myself. But please, fight for this land. I wish to stay here forever."

Liza gradually closed her begging eyes and her body literally turned soulless. Liam gently placed her on the bamboo floor, and when he slowly lifted his head to look straight at his lover's killer, there was fury in his pained face.

The guilty attacker sinisterly smirked and frantically attempted to deeply stab Liam with his sharp dagger. But the healed man was extremely agile and he swiftly clenched the deadly weapon from the desperate killer.

In an instant, Liam fiercely cut the throat of his defeated enemy that immediately fell down lifeless. Liam mindlessly threw the sharp dagger, and when he quickly turned to return to his dead lover, Liza was nowhere.

"Liza?" He uttered in pain.

A strange sound abruptly responded to him, and he gradually noticed small tailed reptiles in the bamboo house. Liam sweetly smiled and spoke with assurance. "You'll always be home, Liza."

Salome the Salmon

A seaside village was formed by concrete houses, protected by obedient families, and ruled by a respectful head. The solid land symbolized the united hearts, and the pristine water signified the loyal souls of the villagers.

The village head was widely known as Mister Felipe who faithfully lived with his longtime and only wife. In spite of decades of countless tries, the power couple remained childless.

However, the villagers constantly prayed for the future parenthood of their village head and his wife, as their strong relationship certainly made the village known for unity and loyalty.

In consecutive ordinary evenings, the power couple desperately made love in their heated and moonlit room. But the aging wife remained deprived of even a single sign of pregnancy.

She steadily stared at her old husband with shame in her eyes. With frustration in her voice, she clearly uttered her painful request. "Felipe, giving you a child is beyond my ability. With my consent, please do sleep with another woman. A young and fertile woman."

With mixed shock and anger in his voice, Felipe emotionally answered his miserable wife. "Do not lose hope, my only missus. The heavens will eventually grant our ultimate desire."

The unconvinced wife swiftly shook her head and sternly insisted. "Prove your love for me, Felipe. Do impregnate a woman in secret. I will treat as my own the child you made with her. And let the woman perish forever."

Felipe completely turned silent as a sign of his submissiveness. His voice calmed as he gently expressed his faithfulness. "I have no eyes for any other women, my missus. I can't choose who to have a child with other than you."

The pained wife surprisingly trembled in a second but rapidly regained her composure. "I will choose for you, Felipe. Tomorrow, in the middle of the night, you alone should welcome her into our room. She is chaste and pure. You'll be the first man inside her being. Call her, Salome."

As Mister Felipe absentmindedly wandered in his village of unity and loyalty, his miserable wife determinedly prepared their room for his set mating with a young and fertile woman.

When the silver moon mysteriously lit up the night sky, the village head quietly returned to his concrete house and sadly felt the physical absence of his beloved wife.

Felipe thoughtlessly entered their romantically scented and renewed room. His confused soul deeply suffered the idea of infidelity and subtly held the anticipation of fulfillment.

All of a sudden, he strongly felt a feminine presence in front of him. Felipe instantly agreed with the clear notion that the woman was a certain embodiment of youth and fertility.

His physical manhood surrendered to manipulative lust, and his masculine voice obsessively called the woman's name, Salome.

In the heated and moonlit room, Salome's chastity was torn apart by the first man in her womanhood. Her purity utterly became a thing of the past as Felipe greedily possessed her every inch and core.

Without their knowledge, the miserable wife jealously observed them through a glass window. She clearly witnessed the sheer pleasure experienced by her domineering husband with a submissive woman.

The infuriated wife crazily ran and screamed around the village of unity and loyalty. The innocent villagers extremely panicked and confusingly rushed to the village head's house to shockingly catch him lustfully possessing a young woman.

Felipe mindlessly froze in shame, and the naked Salome swiftly dashed toward the waving sea. Salome weakly prepared a wooden boat to obviously escape from the chaotic village, but the jealous wife suddenly pulled her.

"How dare you steal my husband?!" The pained wife angrily accused the young woman.

Salome hysterically cried. "You betrayed me! I lost face because of you!"

"Don't you act like a victim! You enjoyed the mating. I told you to give us a child. Not to give Felipe the pleasure that I can never give him!" The miserable wife crazily yelled at Salome.

The silver moon was suddenly covered by dark clouds and the heavy rain violently poured down. Salome and the village head's wife physically fought. When the aging wife weakly lay on the wet ground, Salome quickly returned to the wooden boat.

She desperately tried to cross the violent sea by strongly controlling the oar, but a huge wave mightily turned her boat upside down. Salome instantly failed to emerge from the wild water, and a new species began leaping from the sea, as the village eventually lost its reputation.

Bea the Bee

A young lady timidly walked down a narrow disorderly road that was crowded by multiple vendors. They actively and noisily sold various things from fruits and vegetables, meats and drinks, glasses and metals, to fabrics and utensils.

Despite the dizzying ambience of the working vendors, the young lady steadily held her composure that showed her mastery of the messy place. She mindfully stopped in front of an old woman that meekly displayed small bags of flower seeds.

"How are you, Grandma?" The young lady politely asked.

The old woman delightfully responded. "Oh, here is my regular customer!"

"Yes, Grandma." The lady innocently smiled.

"Come here, Bea. See my new flower seeds." The woman excitedly opened a small bag.

Bea eagerly looked at the seeds. "Do they grow into vibrant and fragrant flowers?"

The woman assuredly nodded. "Yes, they do."

Bea widely grinned. "I'll buy some bags for now, Grandma."

The woman heartily chuckled. "As I expected from you, Bea."

"I really admire flowers. It's better to talk with them than most people." Bea pensively said.

The woman slowly shook her head. "Don't say that, Bea. I'm sure you'll find a person to admire."

Bea casually continued to talk. "I wish that flowers will still exist in the far future. Though I'm no longer alive at that time. So they will carry the stories I'm about to tell them through decades to come."

The young lady happily purchased small bags of flower seeds, and left the busy area of street vendors with a radiant face.

Bea hurriedly walked for a few meters, gracefully arrived in her blossoming garden, and excitedly sowed the flower seeds she newly bought from the old woman.

The thick clouds in the vast sky gradually gathered and darkened her flowery surroundings. Bea confusingly lifted her head to witness the mysterious phenomenon.

"What is happening? Is something coming?" She uttered in fright.

All of a sudden, the heavy clouds dispersed as if hoovered by invisible air, the entire sky glowed like a huge lightning flash, and a thunderous sound forcefully struck the eerie silence.

In an instant, the placid place of blooming flowers returned to its normal condition. Bea was still horrified when she gradually noticed nearby disturbing groans.

She confusingly searched for the unknown source of the painful sound, until her troubled eyes slowly got fixed on the ordinary sight of a tree. She quietly walked towards the nondescript tree, and the repetitive groans steadily loudened.

Bea obviously looked certain about the exact location of the groaning creature, and she abruptly stepped as if to triumphantly catch the unknown thing behind the still tree.

However, she confusingly moved backward upon seeing a male stranger in distinct clothing crawling on the grassy ground.

"Who are you? What are you doing here?" Bea alarmingly stammered.

The male stranger tightly held his sore leg as pain tensed his young face.

"Can't you hear me?" Bea annoyingly asked.

The crawling stranger abruptly stared at her with confusion in his facial expression.

He innocently asked. "What time am I in?"

Bea answered with irritation. "I'm not sure. But it's getting dark now. The night is coming."

The dissatisfied stranger shook his head. "You don't get it."

Bea instantly asserted. "What do you mean? And who are you?"

"I am Neo." The male stranger calmly spoke.

"Neo? This is my first time seeing you. Where are you from?" Bea eagerly asked.

Neo seriously said. "Future."

"What?" Bea uttered in disbelief.

Neo and Bea shyly stared at each other, and their first conversation subtly hinted at their budding mutual attraction.

As days leisurely passed by, they told stories from their different times as they joyously planted flowers that witnessed their growing admiration for each other.

However, after their several shared sweet moments, Neo abruptly grew distant, and Bea shamelessly broke the silence between them.

"What's wrong, Neo?" She asked with irritation.

Neo offensively replied. "It's us! We shouldn't see each other this way."

"Why? What makes us wrong?" Bea continued with pain in her voice.

"I don't belong here. I belong to the future." The emotionless Neo spoke with clarity.

Bea answered with a cracked voice. "No, Neo. You belong to me."

Neo coldly continued. "I am leaving. I must go back to the future."

Bea suddenly cried. "So bring me with you!"

Neo spoke like a stranger he was before. "I'm sorry."

The mysterious phenomenon that unexpectedly brought Neo to Bea gradually unfolded. Horrible darkness surrounded the blossoming garden, and a blinding light instantly followed.

When the tremendous glow abruptly vanished, Neo disappeared. His physical absence powerfully arrested Bea's heart, and her lifeless body fell when a thunderous sound utterly devastated the still silence.

When the blossoming garden looked placid and normal again, the old woman that sold small bags of flower seeds leisurely passed by. She slowly noticed flying insects that were seemingly new to her aged eyes. She pensively nodded her head and eventually left the flowery place.

Tita the Tick

At the fertile mountain vastly filled with fruit-bearing trees, sweet-smelling shrubs, and intertwined vines, the ecstatic newlyweds, Nino and Tita, hastefully arrived in their well-built house. They exclusively savored their honeymoon period as they passionately made love for consecutive warm days and cold nights.

"My love, my Tita, I'll pamper you for the rest of our life together. I'll provide you with every single thing you need and want. Shelter, food, water, warmth, light, and love. Just let me be your one and only man." The husband sweetly promised.

"Yes, my man, my Nino. I'll love you alone. I'll always be your faithful, kind, and soft wife. I'll stay here in the shelter you built for us. I'll always submit to you." The wife obediently replied.

However, despite their consistently intimate relationship, the young husband and wife stayed childless unlike the fruit-bearing trees. As multiple weeks leisurely went by, their concrete shelter gradually turned stale unlike the sweet-smelling shrubs.

The young newlyweds, Nino and Tita, that were comparable to intertwined vines obviously grew cold and strange to each other. Their honeymoon period that was accompanied by sweet nothings drastically changed into their critical period that was prolonged by silent treatment.

Nino regularly yet quietly brought Tita various fresh fruits from his high-yielding orchard. He seemed to eagerly act on his role as the masculine good provider, but he also seemed to intentionally fail his role as the emotionally available husband.

He constantly lay beside Tita in their shared bed, but when she obviously fell into a deep sleep, he silently rose up and secretly went out of their well-built house. Amid consecutive dark and cold nights, Nino hurriedly entered his fruitful and fragrant orchard.

Before the bright mornings disturbingly arrived, Nino alarmingly left his high-yielding orchard and soundlessly returned to pretentiously sleep beside his wife. However, the inevitable time for Tita to finally notice the silent and secret behavior of Nino obviously came.

Tita surprisingly woke up at midnight and instantly noticed the physical absence of her husband. She actively remained awake by simply sitting in their bed, and after a few hours of waiting, the door slowly opened and Nino finally showed up and was caught by surprise.

"Where have you been?!" Tita asked with anger and suspicion.

"I've been from the orchard. Are there any other places I should go to?" Nino calmly replied.

Tita fiercely shook her head. "I don't believe you! How long have you been doing this?"

Nino nonchalantly shrugged his shoulders. "Doing what? I'm not doing anything."

"You promised to provide for me. But where are your emotions now?" Tita asked in pain.

"What are you talking about? I've provided you with shelter and food." Nino said with pride.

Tita suddenly sobbed. "You've been emotionally unavailable. I can't feel you anymore."

Nino strongly raised his hand. "Stop, Tita. I don't need your drama."

Tita cleared her throat and asked. "Are you seeing someone else?"

Nino quickly shook his head. "Stop being too dependent on me. This marriage is suffocating."

"Is that your indirect way of saying yes?" Tita boldly queried.

Nino confusingly looked at his wife and was obviously unable to speak.

Tita nodded her head with certainty. "It's a yes."

After a brief pause, she clearly continued. "I'll give you another chance, Nino. Don't do it again."

Tita hastefully went out of their room that was partially brightened by the new morning. Nino quietly spent the entire day inside their stale house by lying down in their bed. When the night obviously came, Tita silently entered their room and lay beside Nino.

Nino calmly spoke. "We've been married for a few months. It was full of promises and hopes. I did my best for you. I was possessive, perhaps obsessed. And now, you're jealous, accusing me of seeing someone else. And I came to realize, you are the woman I married by mistake."

Tita was painfully shocked by Nino's blunt words, and Nino nonchalantly rose up. Before he physically exited from their shared room, Tita clearly spoke words that sounded like her last.

"I'm sorry for sucking life out of you. I promise you'll never see nor hear from me again when you return. I'm letting you go. Now, you can leave."

Nino calmly shut the door, and when the dark night was obviously taken over by the bright morning, he ecstatically returned with a vibrant woman. He was about to make love with her in the room when he suddenly felt stinging pain around his ear.

His ear abruptly turned itchy as a small bump occurred. He irritably scratched it and he surprisingly held a tiny parasite that was new to his sight. As ordinary days naturally passed by, the parasite seemed to quickly multiply as it became visible almost everywhere at the mountain.

About the Author

Ancel Mondia

Ancel Mondia was awarded Fiction - Woman Writer of the Year by Ukiyoto Publishing in 2023.

www.ingramcontent.com/pod-product-compliance
Lightning Source LLC
LaVergne TN
LVHW041600070526
838199LV00046B/2063